Special Shoes for My Little Feet

Written by Susan D. Powers

Illustrated by Kim Sponaugle

AAE

Text copyright © 2021 by Susan D. Powers

Illustrations copyright © 2021 by Kim Sponaugle

Printed in the United States of America

Published by:
Author Academy Elite
P.O. Box 43
Powell, OH 43035

Paperback ISBN-978-1-64746-394-6

Library of Congress Control Number: 2020913180

I dedicate this book for the love of family;
To parents, all around the world who work hard to create
a strong set of footprints for their children to follow;
To God, for partnering with me in the creation of this
precious little picture book; To Joe, you are my home;
To Makynze, Haydin, and Ashby—you are the joy and
inspiration that become pages in my books.

Boy, Pickles, Daddy sometimes says things I don't understand.
It makes me wonder, though...
Could it be true?

This morning while putting on our shoes, Daddy said, "You know,
Gilbert, our family doesn't just wear ordinary shoes.
We wear *special* shoes."

"Really, Daddy? What makes them special?"

"You do, Gilbert!"

"Me? How?"

Daddy smiled and ruffled my hair. "Because of how important you are."

If that's true, what makes *me* so important?

Is it my red hair
and blue eyes?

Maybe it's my
singing voice.

Is it because I like to build things?

Or maybe it's how good I am at training my pets.

I don't know, but I sure would like to find out.
But how?

Pickles, you're a genius!
I forgot about my family's special shoes.
Maybe if I wear them, they'll show me what makes me so important!

I'll try Mommy's comfy shoes first.
She wears these a lot!

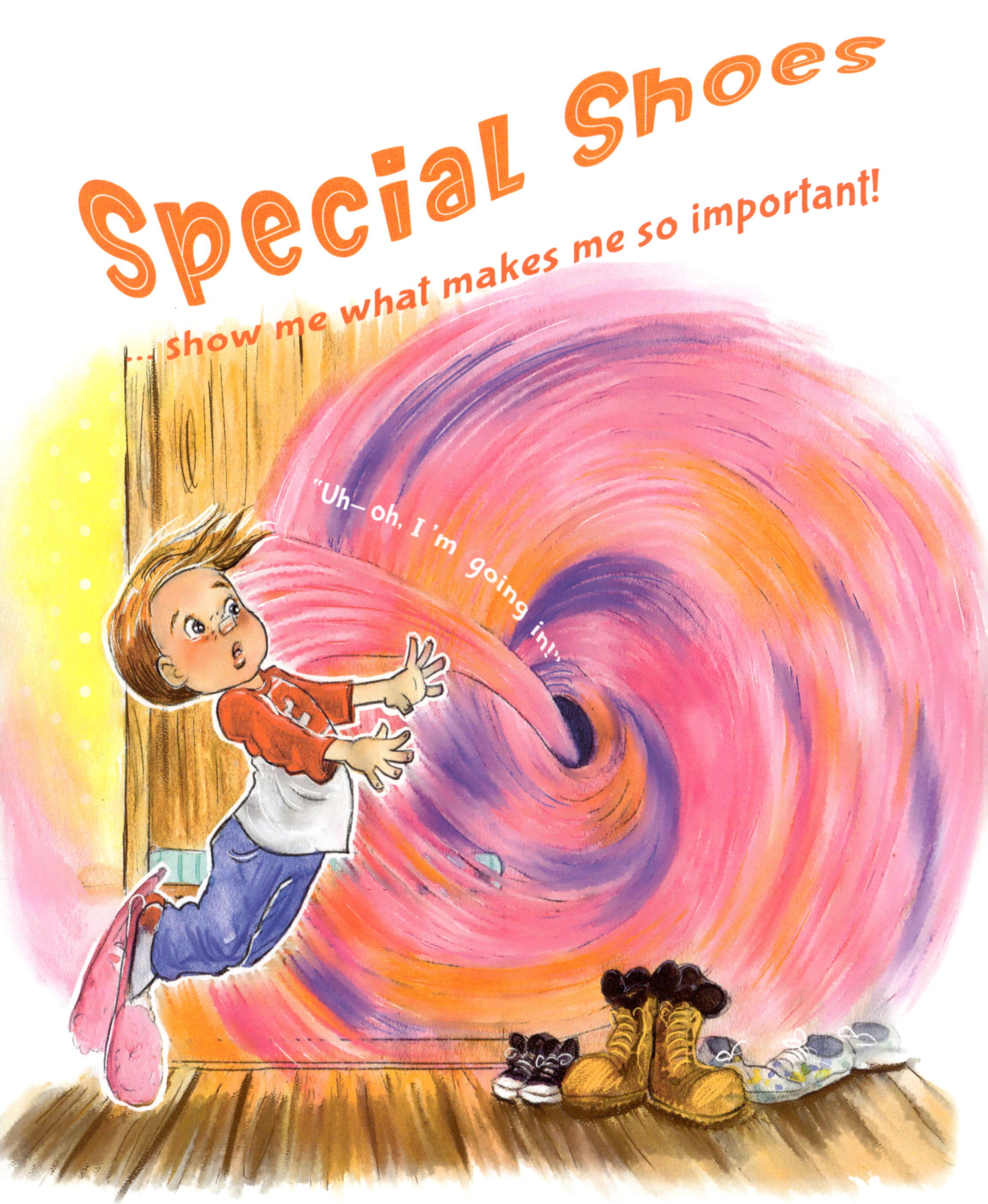

Special Shoes
...show me what makes me so important!
"Uh—oh, I'm going in!"

Hey, I'm in our kitchen.
Oh, it's Mommy's planner.
Mommy crossed out her whole day for me!

I remember Fort Day! We built a castle,
made dragon cookies, and played Enchanted Kingdom.
That was the best day ever!

I wonder what
will happen if I
take off her shoes...

I'm back in the
mudroom!

I'll wear Grandpa's
racing shoes next.
He says they make
the car go faster.

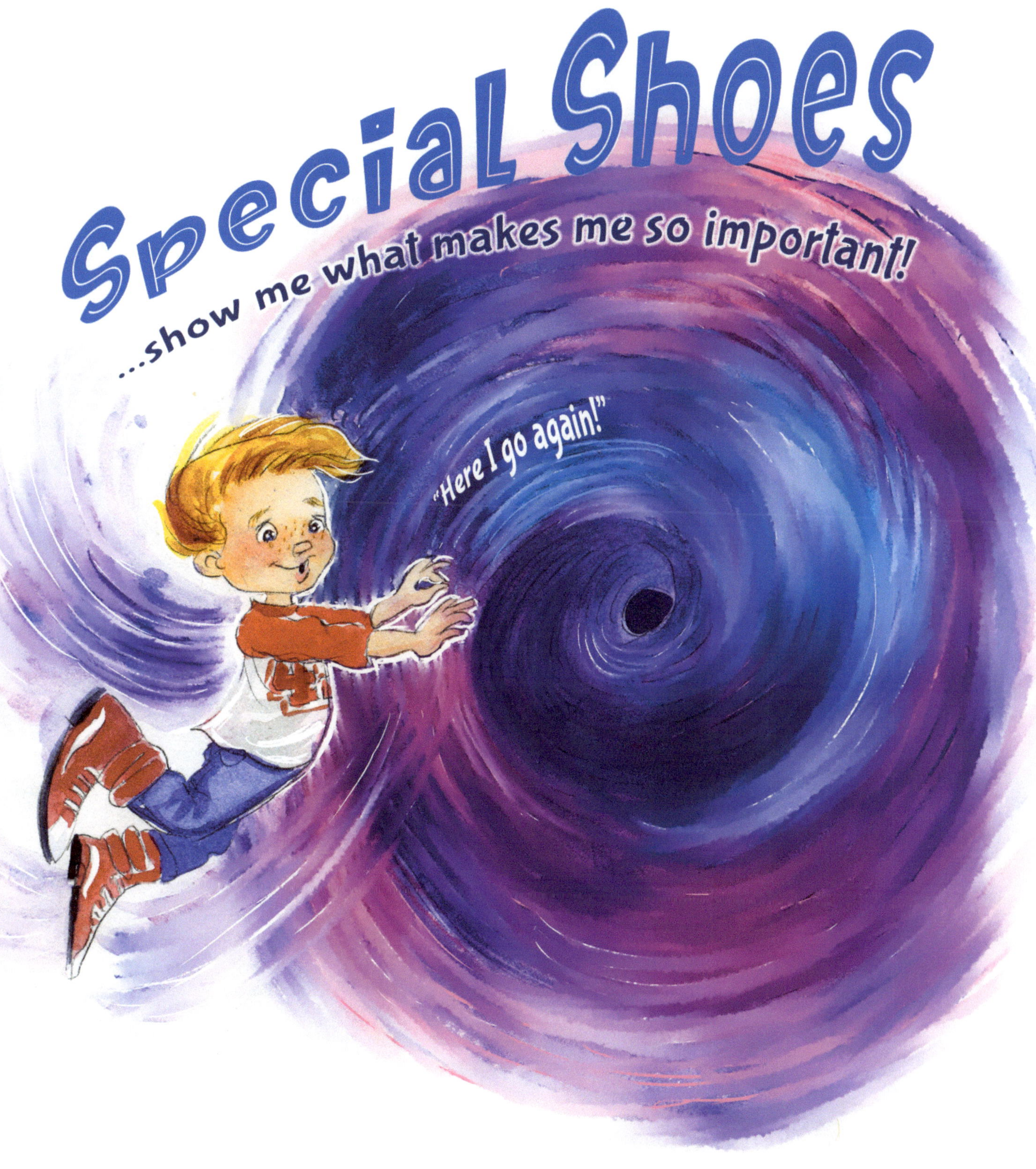
Special Shoes
...show me what makes me so important!
"Here I go again!"

It's Grandpa's workshop!

I know this car.
It's Clyde—the car Grandpa and I built together.

When we finished, we took Clyde to the racetrack.
Grandpa always says, "Hard work equals big rewards!"

Special Shoes
...take me home!
POOF!
POOF!
POOF!

This time I'll wear
Grandma's art shoes.

She's always painting our
adventures together.

Special Shoes

...show me what makes me so important!

Yay! I'm in Grandma's art room!

Hey, a painting is missing from the wall.

Hold on! I don't remember any of these adventures!

Where am I?

Oh, there I am!

Good thing too, because Grandma says we go together like rain boots and mud puddles!

Special shoes...

I wonder what Daddy's work boots will show me.

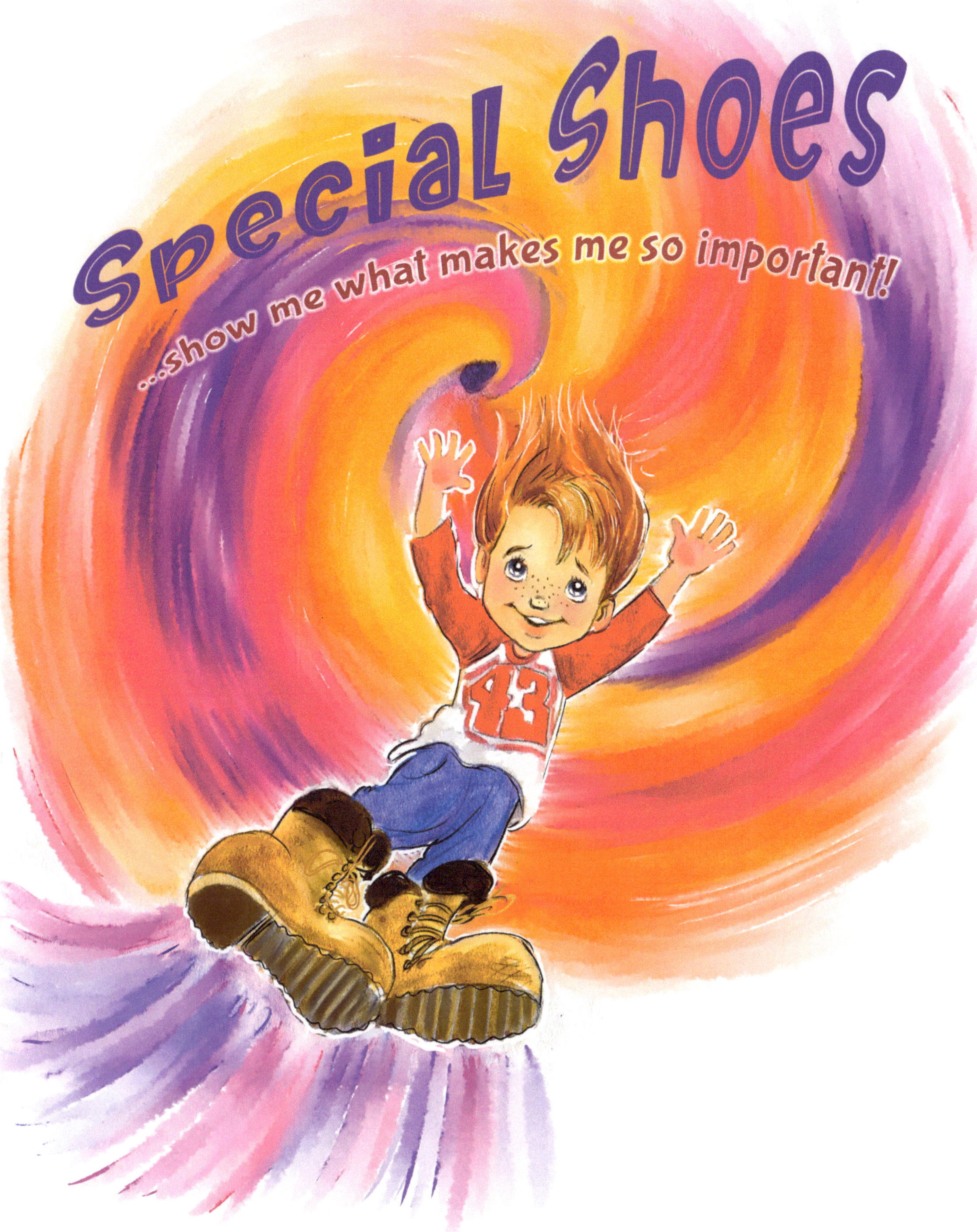

Special Shoes
...show me what makes me so important!
43

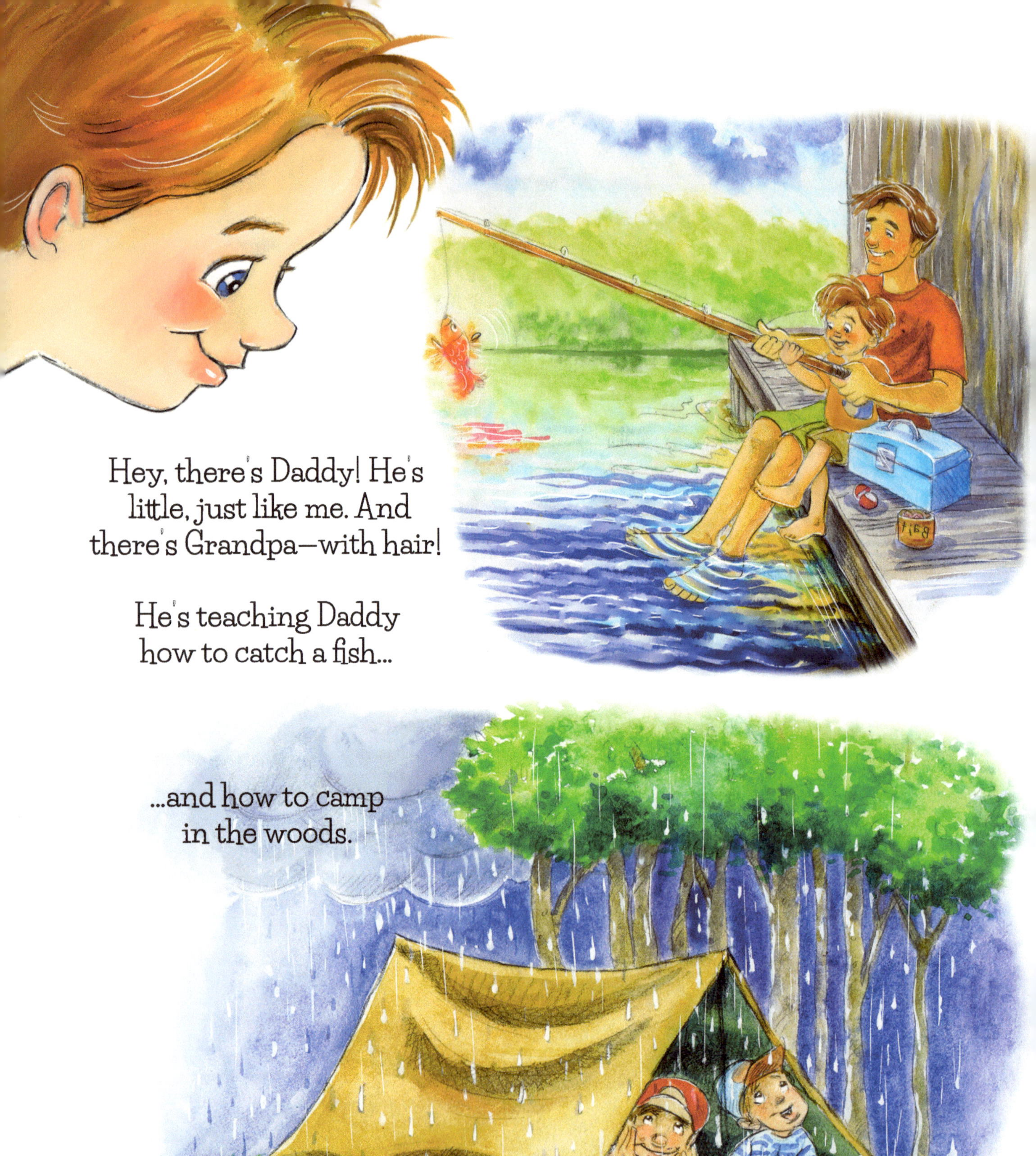

Hey, there's Daddy! He's little, just like me. And there's Grandpa—with hair!

He's teaching Daddy how to catch a fish...

...and how to camp in the woods.

There they are painting the house.

Now they're saying
bedtime prayers.

Wait! Grandpa's teaching Daddy
all the good things that Daddy has
been teaching me.

Now I get it!

Special shoes TEACH
ME good things!

That's why my family
wears them.

That does make me
feel important!

POOF!
POOF!
POOF!

"Gilbert, honey, what are you
doing with all our shoes?"

"They're special shoes, Mommy!
They showed me what makes me
so important."

"That's great, Gilbert.
So, what makes
you so important?"

"My family does!"

Susan D. Powers

"It's the little moments that, if we're paying attention, can create the biggest impact on our lives."

One day, when Susan's granddaughter was about two years old, she came into the kitchen wearing Susan's oversized high heels, proclaiming, "I'm Grandma!"

It was one of those profound moments, as Susan watched her granddaughter proudly stomp around the kitchen in her shoes, that made her stop and consider the question: "Are you happy with the legacy you are leaving your kids and grandkids?" The answer was a resounding...No!

Susan started to look at areas of her life that fell short, and she wasn't happy with the legacy she had created up to that point. So, she began to work on herself—transformational work. She declared that the legacy she was going to leave would create such a positive ripple effect that it would carry through for many future generations to come!

The image of Susan's granddaughter in her oversized high heels never left her, and it made her wonder what else her granddaughter was seeing while wearing her shoes?

Along with Susan's journey to give her children and grandchildren a powerful legacy, the moment inspired her to write a picture book about a child's adventure into the lives of his family by wearing their shoes.

Since the publication of *Special Shoes for My Little Feet*, Susan continues to write for children. She lives with her family and two cats, Leo and Arlo, in Northern California.

Kim Sponaugle

Kim loves to draw stories for kids and comes from a family of animated storytellers.

She has illustrated over 100 books, for both traditional and indie children's book markets, and has the best time working with authors.

When she's not illustrating, you might find Kim watching her tiny hummingbird friends, writing stories, discovering great treasure, and living life with her family in Southern New Jersey.

Author visits available for your class, school, group, or organization.

Scheduling and information at sdpowersbooks.com

Connect on social media at https://linktr.ee/susandpowers